ISBN 978-0-9549715-4-0

Published by

JOHNSTON PUBLISHING (NI)

Esky Drive, Carn, Portadown, BT63 5YY

Text copyright Heather McCarter.
Illustrations copyright Gemma Ramsden 2007.

David and his Wheels go to the Park

The book is dedicated to David
- my inspiration and my life.

David is a special boy with a special chair.

It gets him where he wants to go and talks when no-one's there.

David wants to feed the ducks in the local park.

Mum says she will take him as they always have a lark.

Mummy pushes Charlie Chair
and David enjoys the ride.

They both feel safe and happy
with mummy by their side.

Today is a little wet but they
never mind the weather.

They always have a good time as
long as they're together.

The ducks are very hungry and mum throws down the bread.

But all the pigeons get in the way and eat the bread instead.

Then the ducks fill up their tummies and go off for a swim.

They turn and quack a thank you and David waves at them.

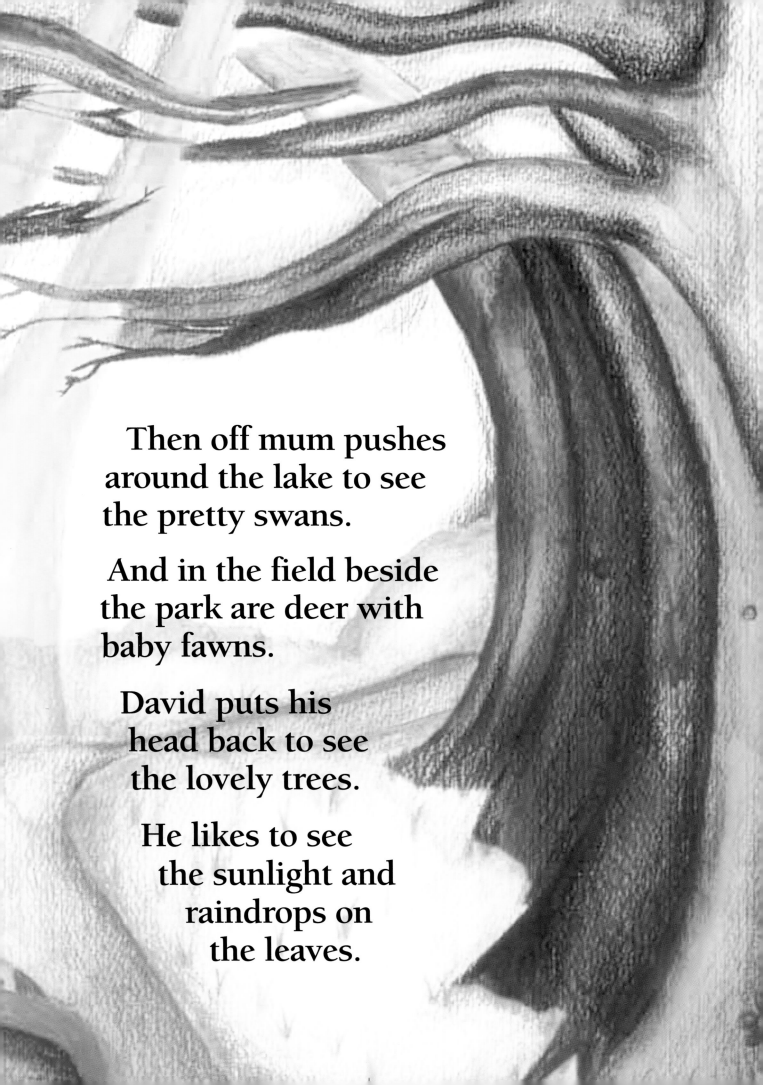

Then off mum pushes
around the lake to see
the pretty swans.

And in the field beside
the park are deer with
baby fawns.

David puts his
head back to see
the lovely trees.

He likes to see
the sunlight and
raindrops on
the leaves.

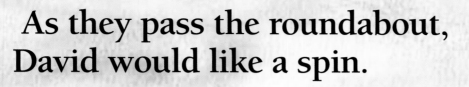

As they pass the roundabout,
David would like a spin.

It's a special one for Charlie Chair
so there's plenty of room for him.

Soon mum decides it's time to go
and David gives a groan.

Up the ramp and into the car,
they're on the road to home.

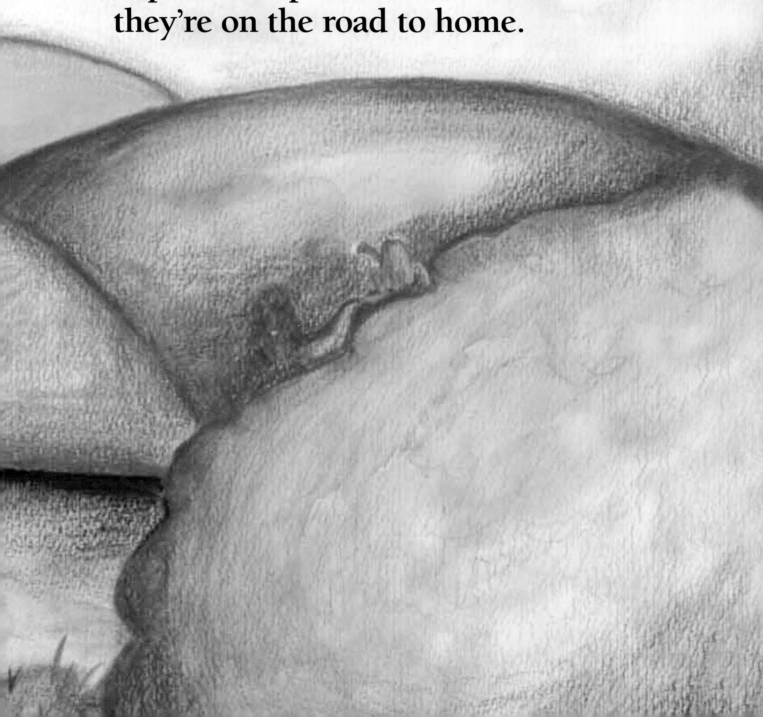

When David is tucked up in his bed,
he and Charlie have a chat.

Then they are joined by Bob,
the family's fat, enormous cat.

Charlie and David would like the
zoo for their next big treat.

Charlie whispers to David
'I'll always be your seat.'

David is a special boy with a special chair.

It gets him where he wants to go and talks when no-one's there.

So next time you see Charlie, with David in his lap, stop and say a big 'Hello'

- they'll both enjoy a chat!